W9-APD-740

# if i was the sunshine

# if i was the sunshine

julie fogliano + loren long

Atheneum Books for Young Readers

New York London Toronto Sydney New Delhi

if i was the sunshine
and you were the day
i'd call you hello!

and you'd call me stay

if you were the winter
and i was the spring
i'd call you whisper

and you'd call me sing

if i was a flower
and you were a nose
i'd call you sniff

and you'd call me rose

if you were a bird
and i was a tree
you'd call me home

and i'd call you free

if i was an apple
and you were a worm
you'd call me lunch

and i'd call you squirm

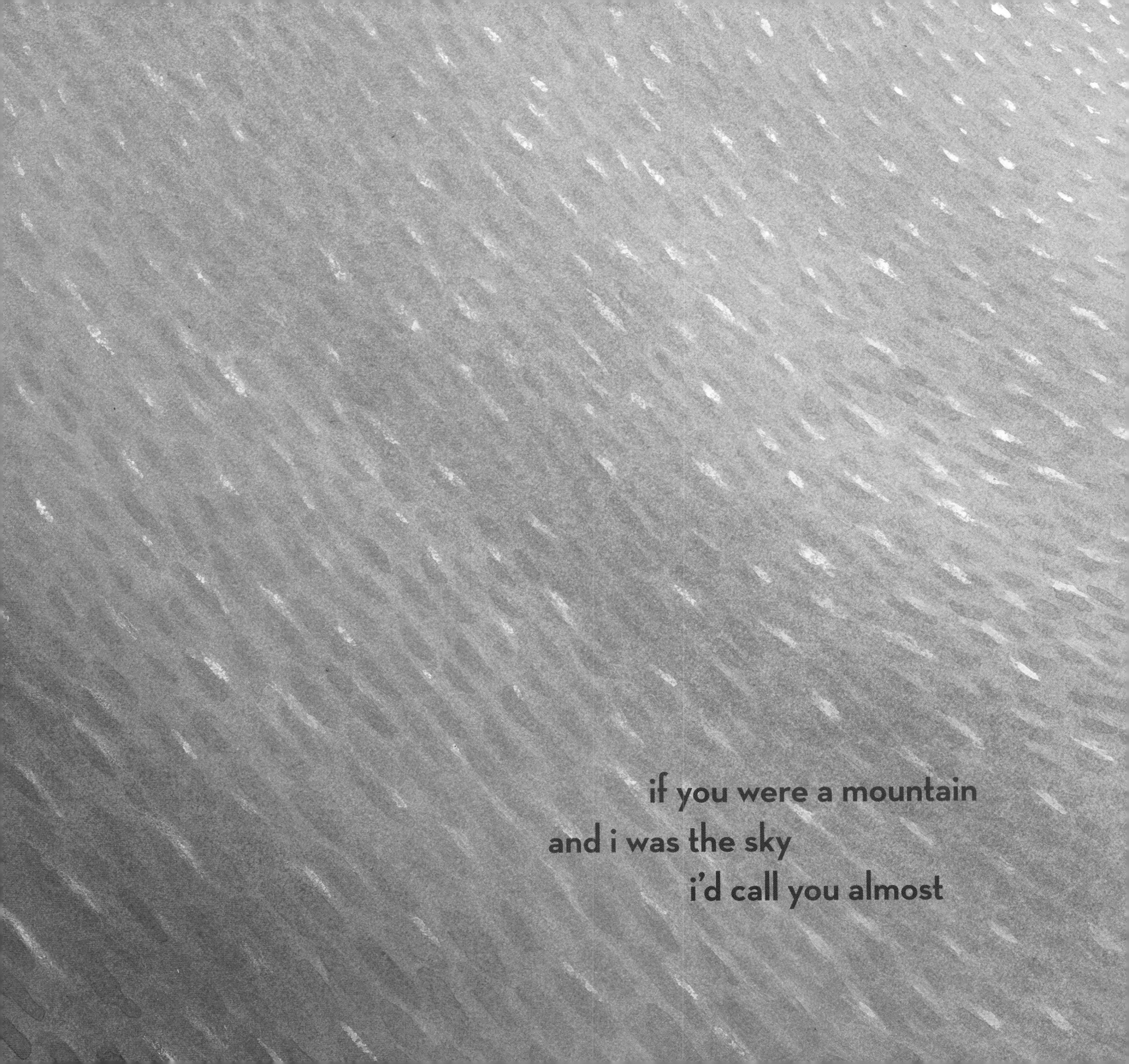

if you were a mountain
and i was the sky
i'd call you almost

and you'd call me high

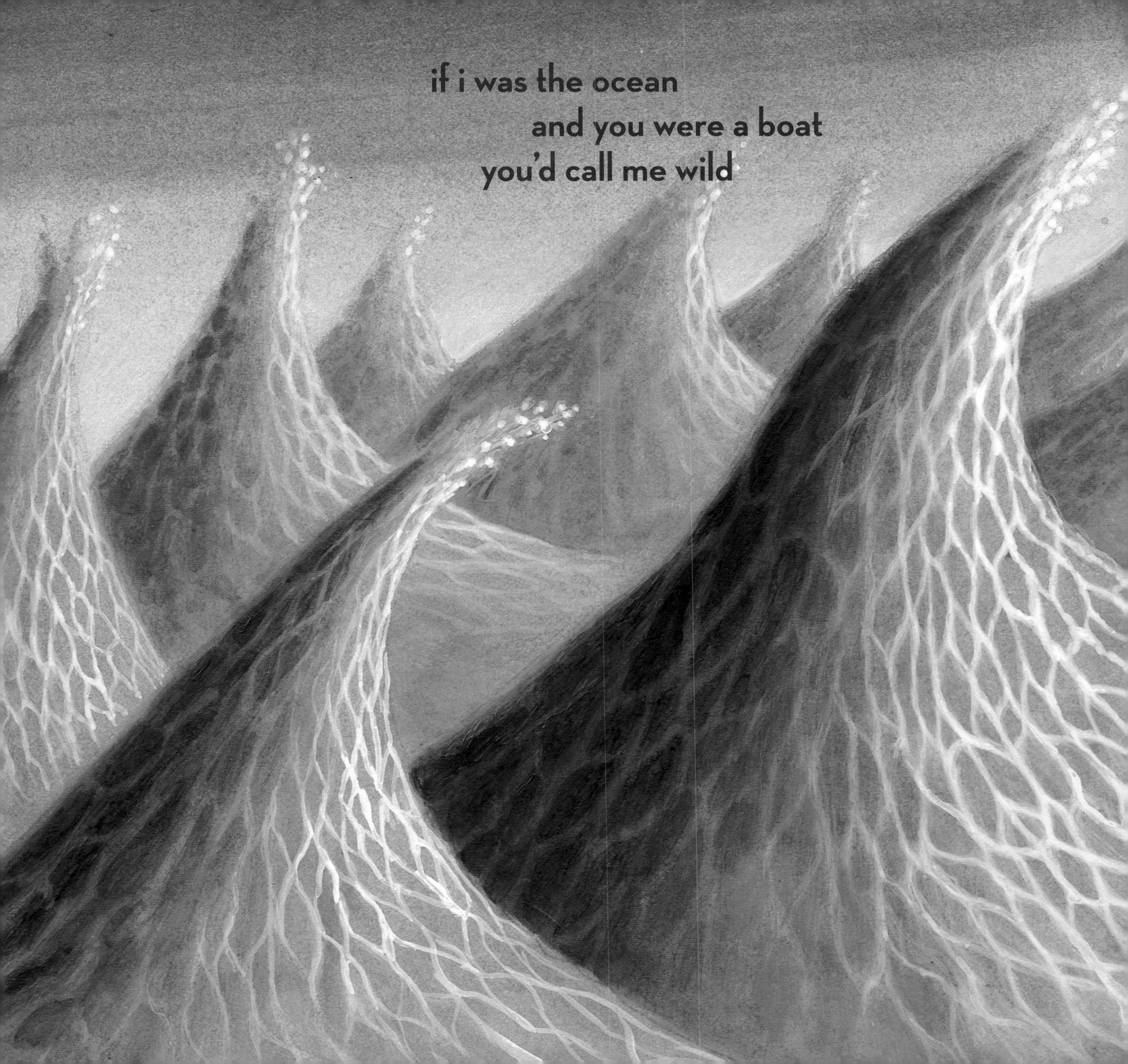

if i was the ocean
and you were a boat
you'd call me wild

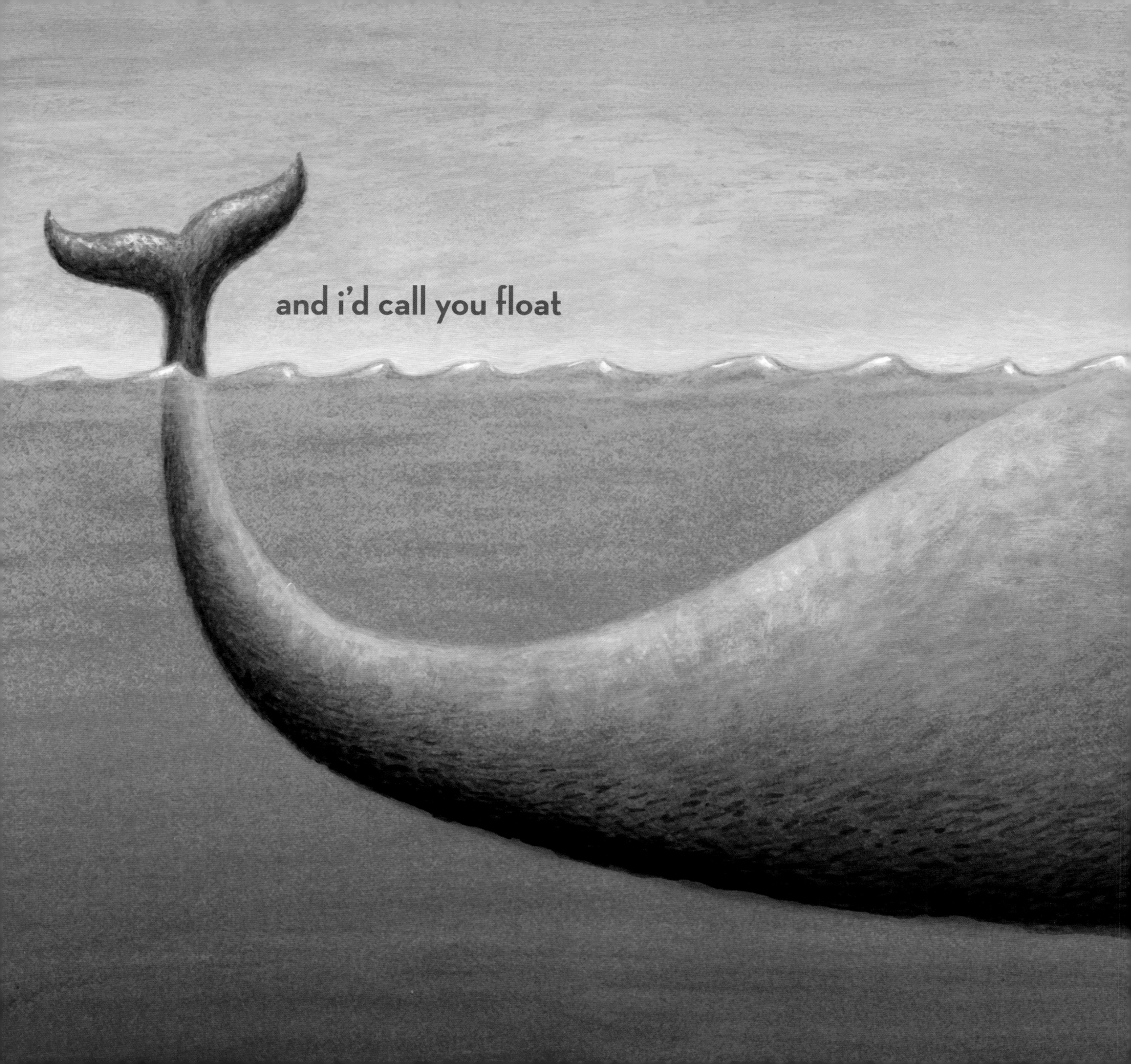

and i'd call you float

if you were the thunder
and i was a cloud
you'd call me softly

and i'd call you loud

if i was the silence
and you were a sound
i'd call you missing

and you'd call me found

if you were a firefly
and i was the dark
you'd call me everywhere

and i'd call you spark

if i was the morning
and you were the night
you'd call me tomorrow

i'd call you
sleep tight

For Eve Jesse
—J. F.

For Moon
—L. L.

atheneum

ATHENEUM BOOKS FOR YOUNG READERS • An imprint of Simon & Schuster Children's Publishing Division • 1230 Avenue of the Americas, New York, New York 10020 • Text copyright © 2019 by Julie Fogliano • Illustrations copyright © 2019 by Loren Long • All rights reserved, including the right of reproduction in whole or in part in any form. • ATHENEUM BOOKS FOR YOUNG READERS is a registered trademark of Simon & Schuster, Inc. Atheneum logo is a trademark of Simon & Schuster, Inc. • For information about special discounts for bulk purchases, please contact Simon & Schuster Special Sales at 1-866-506-1949 or business@simonandschuster.com. • The Simon & Schuster Speakers Bureau can bring authors to your live event. For more information or to book an event, contact the Simon & Schuster Speakers Bureau at 1-866-248-3049 or visit our website at www.simonspeakers.com. • Book design by Ann Bobco • The text for this book was set in Neutraface Display Bold. • The illustrations for this book were rendered in acrylic paint. • Manufactured in China • 0219 SCP • First Edition • 10 9 8 7 6 5 4 3 2 1 • Library of Congress Cataloging-in-Publication Data • Names: Fogliano, Julie, author. | Long, Loren, illustrator. • Title: If I was the sunshine / Julie Fogliano ; illustrated by Loren Long. • Description: First edition. | New York : Atheneum, [2019] | Summary: Illustrations and simple, rhyming text explore the nature of connection and relationships. • Identifiers: LCCN 2018001113 | ISBN 9781481472432 (hardcover) | ISBN 9781481472449 (eBook) • Subjects: | CYAC: Stories in rhyme. | Parent and child—Fiction. | Nature—Fiction. • Classification: LCC PZ8.3.F688 If 2019 | DDC [E]—dc23 • LC record available at https://lccn.loc.gov/2018001113